Acknowledgements

Photographs by Robert Pickett and Papilio Natural History Library.

Contributors: Clive Druett, Jamie Harron, Dennis Johnson, C. Lush, Michael Maconachie, Tony Wilson-Bligh, Peter Worth

The photograph on page 18 is by Mike Read, RSPB Photo Library.

Consultant: Barbara Taylor

The author and publisher would like to thank the staff and pupils of Eardley Primary School, Streatham.

A CIP catalogue record for this book is available from the British Library
ISBN 0-7136-3761-7

Published by A & C Black (Publishers) Limited
35 Bedford Row, London WC1R 4JH

Text copyright © 1994 Kay Davies and Wendy Oldfield
Photographs copyright © 1994 Robert Pickett

Typeset in Univers 16/20pt
by Rowland Phototypesetting Limited, Bury St Edmunds, Suffolk.

Printed and bound in Italy by L.E.G.O. SPA.

Snow and ice

Kay Davies and Wendy Oldfield
Photographs by Robert Pickett

A & C Black · London

In winter, snowflakes fall.

In winter it can be very cold.
Sometimes everything outside
is covered in snow.

If you go out you need to dress up
in lots of clothes to keep warm.
Your hands and feet can get
especially cold.

Look and see how the child in
the picture is dressed.

Which clothes do we wear
on cold days?

Which things keep our hands
and feet warm?

What would you choose to wear
on a snowy day?

Water can turn into ice.

If water gets very cold, it will turn into ice.
When this happens, we say that water freezes.
Sometimes the air is cold enough
for water to freeze.

Look at the picture of icicles.
As water drips from window ledges
and roofs, it freezes and
makes icicles.

You can make ice yourself.
Pour some water into
a plastic bottle.
Put it in the
freezer and wait . . .

What has happened to it
by the next day?

4

Each snowflake is different.

Have you ever seen snow?
Snowflakes are frozen drops of water that fall
from clouds. On the ground, snowflakes stick
together and make a blanket of snow.

Look at the single snowflake.
How many points has it got?

How about the ones in
this picture?

Every snowflake has the same
number of points. But each
snowflake is different from
every other snowflake.

Snow is soft.

Snow is soft. As you walk in it, the snow under your feet gets pressed into shapes called footprints.

Animals' footprints are called tracks. Can you guess what kind of animal made the tracks in the big photograph?

Tracks can tell a story. Look at this picture.

The bird that made these marks was trying to land in the snow. Can you see the shape of its wings in the snow? Can you tell where its feet were?

Ice is slippery.

Have you ever seen a frozen pond?
The ice on top is smooth and slippery.

Birds find it difficult to walk on ice.
Look at the gull in the big picture.
It is trying to keep its balance by
flapping its wings.

You can wear special
boots to walk on icy
surfaces. They have
ridges on the bottom
to help you grip.
(But remember never
to walk on a frozen
pond – it isn't safe.)

Which of these
would you wear
to go walking
in snow and ice?

Ice floats.

Try putting some ice cubes
in a glass of water.
What happens?

Ice is lighter than water,
so it floats.

Icebergs are huge lumps
of ice which float on cold seas.
They can be dangerous
to ships. Sailors cannot see
the part of the iceberg
which is under the water,
and may crash into it.

When a pond has frozen,
can you guess why the ice
is always at the top?

Some plants survive snow and ice.

Some trees lose their leaves before winter arrives.

Although the trees in the big picture look dead, really they are just resting. When spring comes they will grow new leaves.

Many plants die in winter. But some plants survive as seeds or bulbs. They rest underground in the cold soil. When the warm weather comes, they will start to grow.

Put some mustard seeds into two pots of soil. Put one of them in the fridge. Put the other on a sunny windowsill and water it.

What happens to each?

Animals must keep warm.

If you were cold, you might put on another jersey.
Animals and birds can't do that.
Look at the picture of the robin in the snow.
Can you see that its feathers are all fluffed out?
Warm air gets trapped between its feathers.

Before the winter, some furry animals grow
thicker coats. During the winter, animals
spend more time in their nests and burrows
to keep warm.

Can you see this wren
at its nest?

Do you think the wren
would be warm inside
its nest?

Food is hard to find.

It is hard for birds to find food in winter.
The blackbird in the big picture is looking for food
in the snow. Many of the insects and plants
which birds eat die in cold weather. If ponds freeze,
it's hard for birds to find water to drink.

Some birds fly away to
warmer countries for the
winter, where there are
plenty of insects to eat.

You can give birds water
and food. Mix nuts and
seeds with animal fat.
Then put the mixture
into something like this
bell, or half a coconut
shell. Let the mixture set.

Hang it up outside with a piece of string.
How many different birds come to feed?

Snow and ice can turn into water.

When the weather gets warmer, snow and ice turn back into water, or melt.

You can make ice and watch it melt. Find a rubber glove, and pour some water into it. Tie an elastic-band tightly around the top.

Put it in the freezer. Wait until the next morning. Take it out and untie the elastic-band. Ask an adult to help you peel the glove off. You have made an ice sculpture!

Will it melt faster in a warm place? Or a cold place? See if you can find out.

Melted snow waters the soil and seeds sprout.

Look at the river in this picture. The river banks are covered in snow. As the snow melts, more water will run into the river. If the snow melts very quickly, a lot of water will run into the river at once. The river may overflow.

Look at the big picture of a seedling in soil. When snow and ice melt, some of the water soaks into the soil. This makes the soil moist and crumbly, just right for seeds to grow in.

What else happens in spring when snow and ice melt?

Index

This index will help you find some of the important words in this book.

birds	8, 10, 16, 18
clothes	2
floating	12
footprints	8
freezing	4
gripping	10
ice	4, 10, 12, 20
icebergs	12
icicles	4
melting	20, 22
nest	16
seeds	14, 22
snow	2, 6, 8, 22
snowflakes	2, 6
soil	14, 22
spring	14, 22
tracks	8
water	4, 12, 20, 22
winter	2, 14, 16, 18

More things to do

1. Make ice melt faster.
Do you know how to make ice melt more quickly than usual? Make two ice cubes in the freezer. Put each ice cube on a saucer. Cover one ice cube with salt. Which ice cube melts most quickly?

2. Making prints in plasticine.
You can make prints in plasticine. It is soft like snow, and will show the shape of an object pressed into it. Try squashing keys and buttons or string into plasticine. Coins and shells will make good prints too.

3. Sayings about snow and ice.
Talk about the meaning of these sayings.

To skate on thin ice.   To be snowed under.
A heart as cold as ice.   As white as snow.
To break the ice.   To be snowed in.
The tip of the iceberg.

Do you know what this is?

You may see them more often around Christmas time.

Notes for parents and teachers

As you share this book with children, these notes will help you to explain the scientific concepts behind the different activities, and suggest other activities you might like to try with them.

Pages 4, 5

When water freezes it expands. Ice takes up more room than water. A good activity to show this is: put a plastic bottle completely full of water in the fridge with a loose tin foil cap over the top of the bottle. When the water in the bottle has frozen, the ice will lift the cap away from the neck of the bottle.

Pages 6, 7

Snowflakes are made up of six-sided ice crystals. The shape and size of snowflakes depends on the height and temperature at which they are formed and the amount of moisture in the cloud. Looking at pictures of snowflakes provides an opportunity to explore the idea of rotational symmetry. If you make paper snowflakes, you can show children that these snowflakes will still look the same when they are rotated around an axis.

Pages 8, 9

When snow is pressed together, the crystals are crushed to form compacted ice. This happens when you squash snow together to make a snowball. Glaciers in the mountains form in the same way: layers of snow are pressed together to make rivers of ice.

NB The tracks in the picture on page 9 were made by a rook.

Pages 10, 11

The reason why it is easy to slip on a smooth surface like ice is that very little friction is created as you walk. Friction occurs when two surfaces rub against each other. Tiny bumps and holes in the surfaces catch together and make things 'stick' to each other. Without friction, we would slip and fall over every time we tried to walk. The ridges on shoes or boots help create enough friction for us to grip when walking on smooth surfaces.

Pages 14, 15

During spring and summer trees take in water through their roots and lose it through their leaves. A medium sized tree can move 100 litres of water in a day. In winter, trees cannot draw enough water from the soil to replace water lost through their leaves in the normal way. So, in autumn, broad-leaved trees will shed their leaves before the winter weather arrives.

Pages 16, 17

Birds fluff up their feathers in order to trap layers of air between them. Air is trapped between layers of clothing and helps keep heat in in the same way. Several layers of thin clothing will insulate more effectively than one thick piece of clothing. Children can investigate this for themselves by wearing different numbers of layers of clothing.